I LOVE YOU LIKE...

By **Scott Sutton** and **Alec Traub**

Illustrated by **Glenn Zimmerman**

For my son, Alec Sutton,
who makes every day an adventure.
Thank you for asking, "Why?"
- each of the 1.4 million times.
I love you, buddy.
-S.S.

4

5

6

A lot!
Like the
starfish loves
the stars...

7

8

15

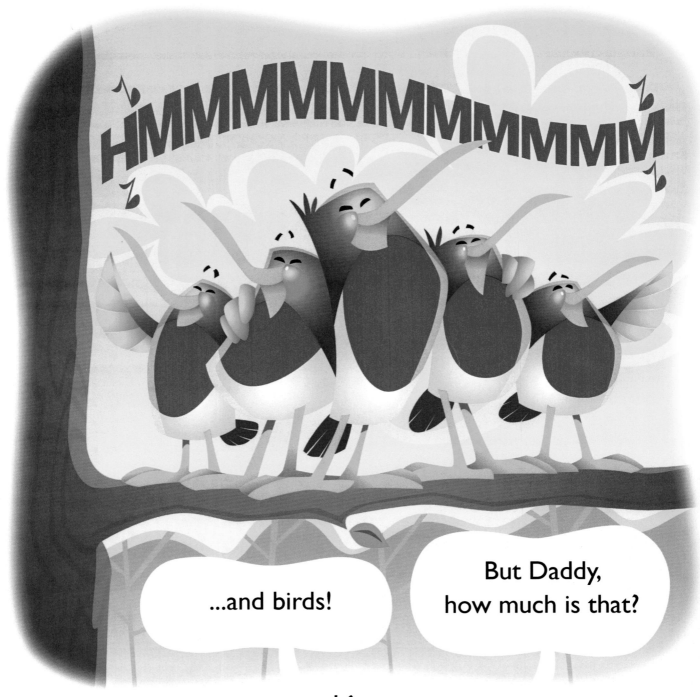

19

21

Made in the USA
Lexington, KY
10 November 2018